# Journey to the Centre of the Earth

Jules Verne
Adapted by Paul Shipton ✳ Dan Baker

OXFORD
UNIVERSITY PRESS

# Notes from the author

*Journey to the Centre of the Earth*, written by Jules Verne, was published in 1864 and was one of the world's first science fiction stories. Of course, the book's scientific ideas about the earth's core are not correct. Nobody could just climb down so far into the earth's core (and even if they could, they certainly wouldn't meet any dinosaurs!). But I don't think this really matters – today, as in Verne's day, readers should think of his story as a fantasy adventure, not as a realistic description of the earth's core.

In adapting the story, I have made a few little cuts and changes. The biggest change is having Graüben join Axel, Hans and the professor on their journey. In the original story she stays at home in Hamburg. I decided that the boys shouldn't get all the fun, and so I let her go on the adventure, too!

Paul Shipton

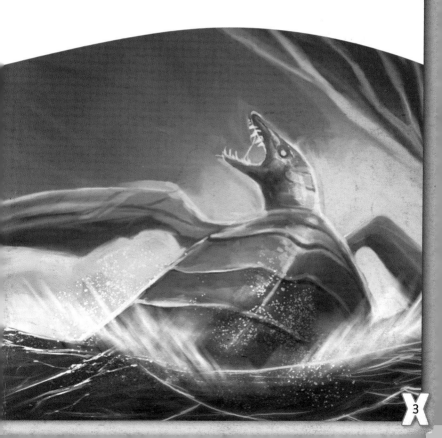

# 1
# Total blackness

I believe I am going to die here in the darkness, far below the surface of the world. But if you are reading these words, somebody must have found my journal. At least people will know of our journey to this incredible place.

But I must write quickly. My light will soon die and leave me in total blackness.

# 2
# The professor

My story begins months ago and many miles away.

One sunny morning in Hamburg, I was at the house of Professor Lidenbrock. He is my uncle and also my employer. The professor is an expert on rocks. Sometimes I think he knows more about rocks than people!

This particular day, he was excited. The reason was an old book he had found in a shop.

"Look at this, Axel!" he cried.

I glanced at the writing in the book but couldn't understand a word.

"It is Icelandic," explained my uncle.

He pointed to a name in ink on the inside front cover. "Arne Saknussemm," the professor read aloud. "He was an Icelandic explorer three hundred years ago. This book was his."

A yellow piece of paper fell out of the book and he bent to pick it up. The columns of letters looked like no language I knew of, but my uncle's eyes grew wide.

"This is a code," he said quietly. "A message from Saknussemm himself! But what does it mean?"

I knew my uncle would not rest until he had the answer. Luckily he knew a lot about other alphabets and languages.

First he changed the characters into the letters as they would be in our alphabet. I wrote the letters down in the same arrangement as he called them out. The words were meaningless.

# 3
# The professor is baffled

Long into the evening we tried to crack the code. We tried many different languages and arranged the letters in various ways.

"What if the letters were written *down* the page and not across it?" my uncle said.

I rearranged the letters again, first writing them down the page and then rewriting them across the page. I hoped their meaning would become clear.

mmessunkaSenrA.icefdoK.segnittamurtn
ecertserrette,rotaivsadua,ednecsedsadne
lacartniiilu)siratracSarbmutabiledmek
meretarcsilucoYsleffenSnl

The professor stared and stared at them.

At last he shouted, "We'll never break this code!"

He stormed angrily out of the house, leaving me alone in the study.

# 4
# Graüben cracks the code!

I was not alone for long.

The door opened and Graüben came in. Graüben's parents had died when she was little. They had been good friends of my uncle and so he gave Graüben a home.

"Why is Professor Lidenbrock so upset?" she asked. Her dark eyes fell on the paper in my hand. "And what is that?"

I started to explain about the secret message, but Graüben interrupted me. "What does *in craterem* mean? It's Latin, isn't it?"

"Yes. It means 'into the crater'. But—"

Suddenly I understood. Graüben had read the words by looking at the back of the paper. She was reading the words backwards!

I began writing the message out in Latin. The professor had been right about the arrangement of the letters – you did have to read them down the page, not across. However, he hadn't tried to read the words backwards. Graüben had found the missing key to the code!

"Can you translate it?" she asked.

"Not very well," I said.

But a voice from the doorway said, "I can."

# 5
# The riddle is solved

The professor was back!

Sweeping up the pen, he translated the first sentence:

**"Go to Iceland and down into the crater of Sneffels."**

"What's Sneffels?" I asked.

"A volcano."

My uncle went on:

**"At the end of June, a shadow will show you the way to the centre of the earth."**

His eyes shone with excitement. For years he had studied and read about what might lie at the centre of the earth. Now he thought he had a chance to see it for himself!

"You must pack our bags, Axel!" he cried. "We're going to Iceland!"

"But how do we know we can believe this note?" I asked.

Graüben was excited, too.

"It's worth trying!" she said. "It will be an adventure! I'll pack my bags, too."

The professor looked at her gravely.

"I'm sorry, my dear. I promised to keep you safe. A trip like this is much too dangerous for you."

Graüben did not answer as she swept out of the room.

# 6
# The journey begins

The following days were a blur of packing and making travel arrangements. I had no time to discuss my worries with the professor, but Graüben could tell from my expression.

"What's the matter, Axel?" she asked.

"Scientists agree that the temperature at the centre of the earth is incredibly hot. How could we travel there?"

"Your uncle is a brilliant man," smiled Graüben. "Don't be surprised if he proves the other scientists wrong." She looked up at me. "But he is not always the most practical. Keep him safe, Axel."

I nodded, wondering why Graüben had not spoken again about going on the trip herself.

Our journey began; first, Germany to Denmark by train. Then, at Copenhagen, we boarded a ship for Iceland. The voyage was rough. Although my uncle was seasick, his face brightened when we spotted Iceland.

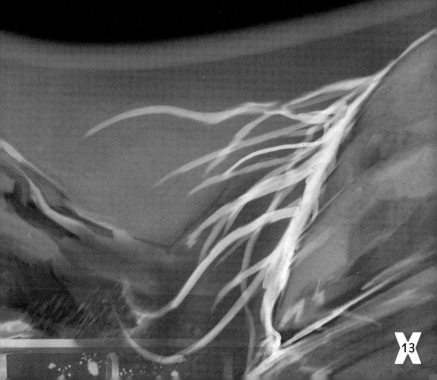

As we neared the rocky coast near the city of Reykjavik, he pointed to a snow-capped mountain north of the bay.

"That is Sneffels!" he announced.

To the professor it was the gateway to the centre of the earth. But the sight of it filled me with fear.

Just then, I thought I heard a noise on the deck behind us. I turned and caught a glimpse of a hooded figure, watching us. But when I turned back again, the hooded figure was gone.

# 7
# The hooded visitor

The final leg of our journey was on horseback, from Reykjavik to the top of Sneffels.

Our Icelandic guide, Hans, accompanied us. He was tall and strong. He didn't speak much, and I couldn't understand him when he did: Hans spoke no German. He and the professor had to communicate in Danish.

On our horses we carried all of our supplies – plenty of food, water, climbing gear, lots of strong rope and head lamps. We also took two rifles and some explosives.

As we neared Sneffels, my mood was as dark as the clouds overhead. I couldn't shake a strange feeling that someone was following us.

The reason for this soon became clear.

As we reached the foot of the mountain, we heard the sound of hooves behind us. Somebody was approaching. I recognized her before the professor.

"Graüben! What are you doing here?" I said.

Graüben threw back her hood and said, "Hello, Axel. Professor." She had followed us to Denmark and then on to Iceland!

Professor Lidenbrock was furious. "You must return at once," he began, angrily.

Graüben shook her head. "I will *not* sit at home and worry myself sick while you have all the fun."

"But our journey is—"

Graüben finished the professor's sentence, "Dangerous. Yes, I know. That's why I'm coming with you – to help keep you safe."

My uncle was an expert on rocks; perhaps he understood that Graüben's determination was as unbending as a rock.

At last he sighed and said, "Very well."

Hans just shrugged.

# 8
# Sneffels' crater

With our horses unable to continue, the four of us now made the long, hard climb up to the top of the mountain. We were soon out of breath. The only one able to speak was Hans, and he chose not to.

My legs ached. It seemed as if we might never reach our destination, but at last we did.

From up there you could look out as far as the sea, but Professor Lidenbrock was more interested in the huge crater at the top of Sneffels.

Lying between the two peaks, it was shaped like a gigantic funnel. It was very wide at the top, but it narrowed to an area of just a couple of hundred metres at the bottom.

"This is madness!" I whispered to myself, as we began to make our way down the slope.

It soon became clear that the professor did not need to worry about Graüben – she was a stronger, faster climber than he was.

After a few hours we reached the bottom of the crater. In front of us lay three deep holes straight down into the rock.

Graüben, Hans and I stared into the terrible blackness of those pits, unable to see the bottom. The professor was looking instead at a large rock to one side.

"Look!" he cried. The name of *Arne Saknussemm* was carved into the rock. "Tomorrow is the last day of June. Then we will learn which hole to go down!"

That night we camped in the crater of Sneffels. All night long I dreamt of black holes and hot lava.

# 9
# Into the earth

Part of me was hoping for a cloudy day, but it was sunny and bright.

At noon exactly the professor saw the sign he was looking for. The mountain peak that rose above us cast its shadow into the crater. At midday, this shadow touched the middle one of the three holes.

"This way!" cried my uncle. "Now for the centre of the earth!"

Graüben smiled nervously, but I felt no enthusiasm. Looking down into that bottomless pit made me dizzy with fear.

Hans tied one of our ropes around a rock and we began the long climb down.

It was slow and difficult work. I lost count of the number of times we pulled down the rope, attached it to a new rock and then lowered it once again into the darkness.

After about twelve hours of this, Graüben shouted. "We've reached the bottom!"

"Is there a way out?" I asked.

It was my uncle who replied. "Yes, there's a tunnel!"

\*　　\*　　\*

The four of us plunged into the tunnel the next day. It was steep but we were able to walk.

My eyes soon became used to seeing only by the light of our head lamps, but this did not ease my worries. The rocky walls of the tunnel seemed to press in on me, and I wondered when we would see the light of day once more.

We did not stop for food until we had gone seven hours.

# 10
# The wrong path?

The next day was the same, until we came to a place where the tunnel forked into two paths.

"Which one shall we take?" asked Graüben.

My uncle thought for a moment, then pointed at one path.

We walked on through arches of hardened lava and rock. The path was not so steep now.

We walked all the next day and the next.

By the light of our lamps we could see the fossils of long-dead animals and plants. But Professor Lidenbrock was silent.

Was he wondering if he had chosen the wrong path? We learned the answer to this question when we reached a huge cavern.

At the far side, we came to a dead end.

"This is the wrong path," my uncle said flatly. "We must go back to the other one."

"But that will take three days!" I exclaimed. "And our water is almost gone!"

On the way back we rationed the water carefully, but we still ran out on the first day.

Soon it hurt to speak, so we trudged on in silence. Each step was more painful than the last. We were half-dead by the time we were back at the point where the tunnels forked.

"We must return to Sneffels while we can," I gasped.

The professor shook his head. "I cannot stop now. I promise that we will find water."

I looked to Hans, but the tall guide just pointed to my uncle and said something in Danish. His meaning was clear; Hans intended to stay with the professor.

Graüben's eyes met mine.

"We have come this far. We have to try, Axel," she said bravely.

# 11
# Water, water!

We went on.

The professor still had the strength to study the many kinds of rock we passed through in the new tunnel.

Myself, I could think of just one thing – water.

And then, to my amazement, Hans's deep voice echoed from up ahead. "Vatten!"

Though I did not speak his language, I understood this. Water!

We ran to join the guide, all grinning like schoolchildren. Through the granite in the side of the tunnel we could hear the dull rumble of an underground river.

Hans took his pickaxe and swung it at the rock wall. He did this for over an hour. He never seemed to tire.

Suddenly a jet of water shot out of the hole.

"AH!" cried Hans in pain, jumping aside.

The water was boiling hot!

"Don't worry! It will cool," my uncle said.

He was right.

Water continued to pour into the tunnel and soon we took our first drink in days. Nothing had ever tasted better!

The professor smiled and pointed down at the water at our feet.

"The stream flows downwards – it will act as our guide."

# 12
# Following the stream

And so we pressed on, now following the stream down. We did this for days.

The world above, with its sky and trees and cities and light, seemed no more than a dream. Our world was one of rock and darkness.

At regular intervals, Professor Lidenbrock calculated our position.

"We are now 125 miles south-east of our starting point," he declared, "and 18 miles underground."

I gasped. "That means …"

Graüben finished my thought. "The Atlantic Ocean is above us!"

But we weren't done yet.

We followed the tunnel deeper into the earth. Soon we were 20 miles below sea level, then 30. Still we didn't stop.

At times the tunnel was so steep that we had to use the ropes.

On one stretch like this, it was my turn to go first. Gripping the rope tightly, I climbed down the rock wall.

Suddenly I stopped.

"What is it?" Graüben asked.

"My ears are playing tricks," I said. "I can hear the sea."

"I hear it, too," said Graüben.

Before I could reply, the rock seemed to fall away from my feet – we had come to the end of the tunnel!

As I kicked wildly, I lost my grip. I fell, but it was not for long and I did not hit hard rock below.

Soft sand broke my fall.

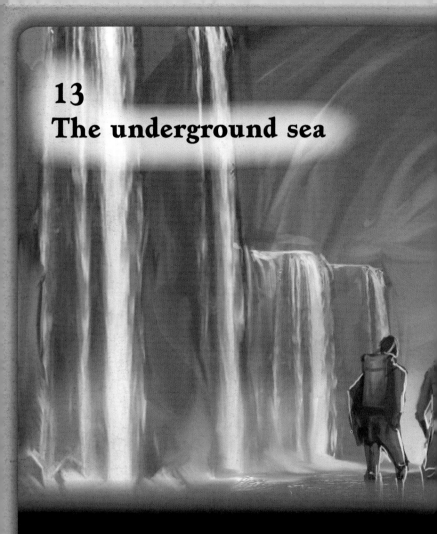

# 13
# The underground sea

The four of us stood on the beach – yes, a beach!
– and looked out in utter amazement.

A cool breeze hit our faces.

We were inside a cave, but this was a cave big
enough to contain a sea. In front of us water
stretched as far as the eye could see.

We did not need our head lamps – the landscape was lit by a glowing light that was neither sun nor moon. Professor Lidenbrock speculated that this must be some kind of natural electricity.

To one side of us, waterfalls cascaded down towering cliffs.

Further along the shore there was a forest, but we soon discovered this was not made up of trees. They were giant mushrooms, each as tall as a house.

There were other plants on the far side of this strange place – pale forest ferns and cacti. They were all bigger by far than those on the surface.

"We have to go back, tell the world about this place," I said.

The professor remained silent.

Behind him, Hans was already starting to cut down giant reeds with his axe.

"We must go on," said my uncle. "We will set sail and learn what lies on the other side of this sea."

I saw a flicker of worry in Graüben's eyes.

The raft was ready the next day. Hans had tied the reeds together with our ropes and made a sail from a sleeping rug.

And so, on Thursday August 13th, we set sail on what we now called the Lidenbrock Sea.

We travelled fast, passing giant strands of seaweed, but there was no sign of land that day or the next.

Our food supplies were running low now, so Hans baited a hook with a bit of meat. Soon he was reeling in a fish.

The professor studied it carefully.

"This fish has been extinct for millions of years!" he declared.

It was a fascinating scientific discovery … and soon a tasty meal!

# 14
# Strange marks

A couple of days later, with still no sign of land, Hans tied a pickaxe to a long rope and dropped it over the side. This was the professor's idea, to measure the water's depth.

But when Hans pulled the rope up, there were strange, deep marks on the axe head.

"Tander," said Hans.

"Teeth," said Graüben.

But what terrible creature could make such tooth marks?

Two days later, I received my answer.

A great bump from beneath us woke me.

Hans pointed to a great dark shape in the water. It was less than half a mile away. A huge creature of some kind!

Its back rolled in and out of the waves. Then its huge head broke the surface.

It looked like a giant lizard with a porpoise's snout and crocodile teeth as long as daggers.

"An ichthyosaurus!" exclaimed Professor Lidenbrock. "The most fearsome of the sea dinosaurs!"

I had the rifle to my shoulder, but Hans shook his head. He was right – bullets could not harm such a monster. Our only chance was to flee before it saw us.

# 15
# Monsters!

We could sail the raft well now, and we changed direction quickly.

I looked back at the dark shape of the ichthyosaurus. It still hadn't seen us. Now if we could only sail a little further away …

Suddenly the professor let out a cry.
I looked ahead of the raft and saw a second giant monster of the deep. This one was a giant serpent with the shell of a turtle – a plesiosaurus. It was coming our way.

Panic gripped us.

What chance did we have, with terrible beasts in front and behind us? Either could have

destroyed our little raft with ease.

We were done for.

A half-remembered fact stirred in my mind.

I lifted the rifle again and fired back at the ichthyosaurus.

"No use!" my uncle shouted, but I fired again. I wasn't trying to hit the creature. I wanted to attract its attention.

On my third shot, it turned its head our way and let out a dreadful screech. "Hold on!" I shouted to the others.

The long neck of the plesiosaurus rose high above the raft, but the creature was not about to attack us. It had seen the ichthyosaurus, which was cutting through the water towards it.

These two creatures were deadly enemies!

# 16
# The battle

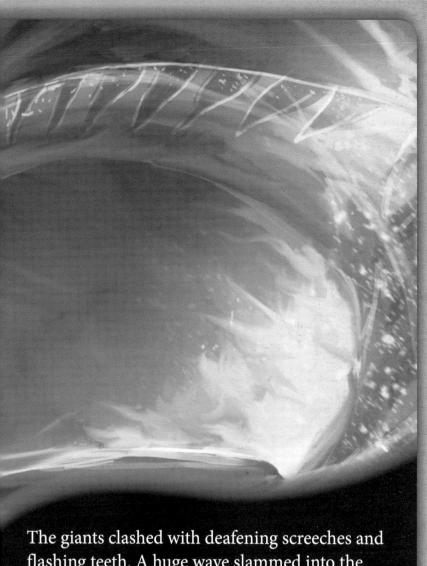

The giants clashed with deafening screeches and flashing teeth. A huge wave slammed into the raft. The next instant, the creatures disappeared under the water. When they reappeared, we had put some distance between us. The two monsters continued to splash and writhe as they fought.

We were too busy trying to steer the raft away to watch the battle, but soon there came a terrible cry.

The plesiosaurus's huge neck waved in the air and then fell. It had lost.

We saw a flash of the ichthyosaurus's tail as it disappeared under the water.

There was no further sign of it, but hours later I still worried that it was about to burst out of the water in front of us.

# 17
# A new danger

After the battle, we spotted other huge sea creatures. Every time this happened, my heart thudded in panic, but the monsters always remained at a distance.

More days passed as we sailed mile after mile.

My uncle seemed lost in thought now. Was he thinking the same as me – what if he was wrong about sailing the underground sea?

We had been on our raft for over a week when we encountered a new danger.

The wind had become stronger and stronger. Sometimes it would stop altogether, then return with the force of a hurricane.

At times like this there was nothing we could do but hold on and trust Hans's workmanship.

There was so much electricity in the air that my hair stood on end.

Hans spoke. The professor translated, "A storm is coming."

It came faster than we feared. One moment the zigzags of lightning were in the distance; the next, they were all around us. They came hurtling down, then bouncing back up to the ceiling of this vast cave.

The four of us clung on to the mast as great waves hurled our raft up and down and hailstones struck us.

I didn't think the storm could get any worse, but it did.

A huge ball of electric fire rolled across the raging waters towards us. It struck our raft in an explosion of blue flames and afterwards our mast was gone. Now we were completely helpless.

"What's that noise?" shouted Graüben.

At first I heard only the endless waves smashing against us and the sizzle of lightning. But then I too heard it – the sea breaking on rocks!

"We are near the shore!" I cried. The last thing I remember is the raft hitting something.

Then my body fell into the water. My head struck something. Unconsciousness swallowed me up.

Of the raft and the fate of the others, I know nothing.

# 18
# Alone

I awoke alone on a rocky shore. How long had I been there? Long enough for the storm to have died down.

I could see no sign of the raft. I shouted the names of my companions again and again. No answer came. Was I the only survivor?

I could not say how long I walked along the shore. I know only that to my aching body it seemed that I had been walking forever.

At last I came to a thick line of ferns. They led to a tunnel set in the cliffs. Which way should I go now? Thinking that I couldn't give up on my companions yet, I turned away from the tunnel and pushed my way through the ferns. I found myself looking out onto a large open plain.

Not far in front of me lay the bones of a large creature. It was a mastodon, a kind of prehistoric elephant with huge tusks. I did not know this by studying the bones; I knew it by looking up and seeing something even more amazing in the distance – several living mastodons, moving across the plain!

Creatures like this had not walked on the surface of the world for thousands of years!

I moved forward for a better view, when I noticed something even more incredible …

A man! At least, it looked like a man but he was over three metres tall.

His hair was long and tangled, and he held a huge branch in one hand. He seemed to be watching over the mastodons as if they were his herd.

Was he really human or was he just an animal who looked human? I will never know.

In the next instant, the giant turned and his eyes met mine. He let out a shout of fury and started towards me.

Without weapons, I knew I stood no chance against such an enemy.

I turned and ran. I could hear footsteps behind me and a murderous cry. I did not look back.

I crashed through the ferns and straight into the tunnel. Was it too big for the giant man to follow me? I couldn't be sure, but I ran on.

After I had felt my way around two or three corners, I stopped and turned my head lamp on.

There was no sound of anything chasing me.

I forced myself to walk on, thinking that I might find an alternative way back to the shore.

I walked and walked.

Shadows from my head lamp danced on the tunnel's rock walls. There seemed to be an entire network of tunnels here, and I tried to keep track of the different paths and entrances.

# 19
# Dead end

After many hours of walking, I came to a dead end. I forced myself not to give up hope. Retracing my steps, I tried another way, but eventually came to another dead end.

Panic stirred within me, making me careless. As I rushed to find a better path, I stumbled and fell. Pain exploded in my leg as I struck the rock. I could barely keep conscious.

I tried to make myself comfortable on the hard rock, but after a few hours I still couldn't put my weight on the leg.

I finished the final rations of food in my bag. Then I decided to write this account of our journey.

My light will not last long and I will be alone in the dark. I wish only that I could be sure my companions are safe, that I could see Graüben's smiling face again.

# 20
# Alive!

I did not die! My head lamp did indeed go out. With no way to measure the passing of time, I do not know how long I sat alone in the darkness. My despair was as complete as the blackness around me. But then I heard an amazing thing – the far-off crack of a rifle!

"Uncle!" I shouted at the top of my voice. "Graüben! Hans!"

The silence seemed to mock my hope. I knew that a rifle shot could carry much further than the loudest shout. However, I did not give up. I counted for a minute, then I shouted again. I repeated this over and over. My voice was hoarse, but this was my only chance.

And then, at last, I heard it – a faint cry in the distance.

"Axel!"

It was my uncle's voice!

"Help!" I shouted.

The next reply was a little louder – they were coming closer!

We carried on this way for a long time, with them getting nearer and nearer. "Where are you, Axel?"

"The tunnels!"

Their voices were coming to me from a sinkhole a little further back down my tunnel.

With great effort I dragged myself towards it, forcing myself to ignore the pain in my leg and my weakness from lack of food.

I realized how lucky I had been. Instead of taking me away from the underground sea, this tunnel had led to another stretch of shore. The hole in front of me now led back down. Its shape meant that it had carried sound from below and amplified it into the tunnel. Only this had allowed us to hear each other.

Finally, I heard my companions' voices much more clearly.

"Can you move?" shouted my uncle. "Follow my voice."

Feeling my way into the blackness, I started to crawl.

The slope down was steep. It became steeper, but soon I could see a dim light. With one last effort, I hauled myself forward towards it and fell into Hans's waiting arms.

My companions' smiling faces were the greatest sight I'd ever seen.

# 21
# A.S.

After some food and water I was feeling better. I learned what had happened after the storm. The others had managed to stay on the raft. After they came ashore, they had concluded that I was dead.

They had explored the shore further, looking now for a way home. When a group of the giant human-like creatures threatened them, Hans had shot the rifle into the air to scare them. This had saved me!

Hans made a crutch for me and I was soon able to walk. I was still practising this when Graüben came running back from the nearby cliffs.

"Come and see!" she shouted.

By the time I joined the others, they were near another tunnel, looking at a rock by the side of the entrance.

Two letters had been carved into it: A.S.

"Arne Saknussemm!" gasped my uncle. "He came this way!"

It was hard to believe that we were still following the Icelandic explorer's route.

Lighting our last head lamp, we ventured into the tunnel. We didn't get far before we came to a huge boulder.

"There's no way round it," said Graüben.

My uncle studied the boulder.

"It must have fallen here after Saknussemm's journey."

We looked at each other. Was our journey at an end?

No! After all we had been through, I wasn't going to turn back.

"We've still got the explosives, haven't we?" I asked. "We'll blow this boulder out of the way!"

No one said anything, but Hans was grinning from ear to ear.

# 22
# BOOM!

We dug a hole big enough for our entire stock of gunpowder. Then Hans ran a long fuse back to the shore.

The water came close to the cliffs here, and so we agreed that the safest place would be back on the raft, which Hans had rebuilt.

Hans lit the fuse and joined us on the water. We watched the small light of the fuse nearing the tunnel.

"What if it doesn't work?" Graüben asked.

I had other worries. Looking back out to sea, I was sure I had seen a big dark shape coming near. Was the ichthyosaurus back?

The next few seconds were unbearable. The shape in the water loomed closer and closer.

Then suddenly – BOOM! – a deafening explosion tore through the air as the gunpowder ignited. Our raft was pushed back. But then the waters around us began to rush forward, carrying us along into the tunnel. With the boulder out of the way, we were swept down into a wide shaft.

We clung to the raft's mast in terror, listening to the roar of water as we fell further and further down. It was a miracle our raft didn't smash to pieces against the sides.

Then an amazing thing happened.

"We are going up!" Graüben shouted.

Hans turned on his head lamp. It was true – we were in a narrow shaft and we were going up.

"The sea reached the bottom of the pit," my uncle explained. "Now it is going back up, and us with it!"

One thing was clear. It was getting hotter and hotter. The water under the raft was boiling!

We were moving upwards at an incredible speed now. It became harder to breathe, because the air was full of steam and then smoke.

Looking over the side, I saw that it was no longer water beneath us but lava!

"We're going to die!" cried Graüben.

I held her hand tightly and waited for the worst.

But then, high above us, I saw a tiny circle of light. We were moving towards it at high speed. Suddenly I understood.

# 23
# Inside the volcano

"We're inside a volcano!" shouted my uncle above the din. "It's taking us back to the surface!"

But how could we survive if we were blasted out of a volcano?

There was nothing we could do now except hold on tight as the raft spun round and round.

The blistering air stung our eyes and burnt our lungs as we tried to breathe. Then suddenly there was a bright light all around us and a rush of cool air.

And then we were falling.

"This is the end," I thought, and I closed my eyes.

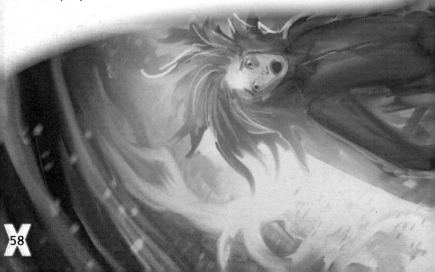

# 24
# Our journey ends

I awoke to sunshine. My companions were unharmed, too. Again we had cheated death.

Sitting up slowly, I found I was on the slope of a volcano. But this place looked very different from Iceland: it was warmer, with olive groves and grape vines.

I later learned we were on Stromboli – an island off the coast of Sicily. We had entered the earth by one volcano and come out of another, thousands of miles away!

As he laughed, Hans was making more noise than I'd ever heard from him. My uncle joined in.

I knew the professor could not wait to report his findings to the world.

As we walked down the mountain, we met a local boy. I knew that we must be a strange sight, walking down from the volcano.

This lad said something in Italian, and my uncle replied in the same language.

"What did you say?" I asked.

"He wanted to know where we came from," answered the professor with a proud smile. "So I told him – we have come from the centre of the earth!"

# Writing tips from the author!

**How did you decide which bits to keep and which bits to change from the original story?**

This adaptation is so much shorter than the original book that it was a matter of squeezing in as much of the story as possible while trying to keep it readable. I only made one big change, apart from letting Graüben go on the adventure. I think one of the best bits of Jules Verne's novel is when Axel is lost and alone far underground. I wanted to start the book with this scene and have Axel tell the story so far. But for this to work, I had to move this event a little later than it is in Verne's novel.

## How does adapting a story compare to writing your own story?

It's a nice change - sometimes a completely blank page can be a bit scary, but you don't get that with an adaptation.

## Where do you usually get your ideas from when you write a story?

I'm afraid where I get my ideas from is something of a mystery to me. I think the important thing is how you develop them.

## What do you think is important to make a good story?

I think the most important thing is getting your reader to care about what happens next.

## What should you remember when creating characters?

Nobody's perfect – and if they were, they'd be pretty boring! I think the most interesting characters have got a flaw or two.

## Do you have a routine for writing?

Not really, but I should!

## Any other tips for writers?

I don't know any writers who don't also read a lot.